CW00495370

This book is dedicated to all those boys and girls who dream up stories, write and draw pictures imagining the world from a wonderful point of view

keep dreaming, writing and drawing, create your own books!

Once upon a time, in a dark and damp sewer hidden beneath the bustling city, there lived a small rat named Pat. He spent his days scurrying through the maze-like tunnels of the sewers searching for food scraps and avoiding the occasional splash of dirty water. Life was boring, and Pat wanted something extraordinary to break the monotony.

The other rats did not like him because he looked, almost, like a mouse rather than a rat. He felt it didn't matter though, he wanted to be part of a community and was looking to make friends with other animals.

One fateful day, while exploring a particularly gloomy section of the sewer, Pat stumbled upon a peculiar sight, a shimmering portal glowing with vibrant colours. Curiosity overcame his caution, and with trembling whiskers, he carefully approached the portal. Its colourful glow summoned him, promising a world beyond his wildest imagination where, maybe, he would meet others and not be alone.

Summoning his courage, Pat took a leap of faith and darted through the portal. In an instant, he found himself in a completely different realm, the Rat Realm. It was a place of enchantment and wonder, where the frozen-over meadows stretched as far as the eye could see. Pat stood there in amazement. Trees adorned with sparkling crystals swayed gently in a soft breeze, casting mesmerizing patterns of light on the ground.

Pat soon discovered that the Rat Realm was home to the most superior rats, who possessed extraordinary abilities. They were intelligent, resourceful, and lived harmoniously, each contributing their unique talents to the community. As Pat explored the Rat Realm, he encountered rats with skills he had never seen before, rats who could weave complex spells, rats with heightened senses, and even rats who could communicate with the spirits of nature.

Their houses were warm, and they didn’t care about the cold, or how each other looked, they were a community.

But the Rat Realm was about to be thrown into chaos. One day, a group of rats emerged from another portal, the rats appeared to be very different. Dressed in gleaming space armour and futuristic helmets, they were rats from a future Rat Realm. These time-traveling rats, led by Captain Roy, warned of an approaching threat, a massive ice storm that would freeze their beloved realm forever. They had travelled back in time to help.

In a flurry of excitement, the rats of the Rat Realms came ogether, uniting their powers and knowledge. They devised a plan to build a machine that could change the weather and move the storm away. Day and night they worked, creating the machine with salvaged materials, adding space crystals to power it with magical energy. The storm arrived and the machine generated a bright light, wind flying out the machine made the ground rumble. The light and wind swept the storm away, changing the sky into sunshine which made the snow melt temporarily around them.

They all became excited, having saved the Rat Realm, but then one of the rats said, “oh no, look!” pointing to where the rats of the future and Pat had once entered. The portals had collapsed. They now had no way of returning home, Pat was stuck too. Captain Roy of the future rats said, “we can get back if we build a spaceship and use our space crystal to time-travel forward”.

Off they went again, using their skills to build another machine, a space craft which could get the rats back. Working as a team and supporting each other, they were happy working.

As the icy grip of the frozen planet tightened, the super spaceship stood proudly, ready for its first voyage. The moment had come for the rats to embark on their grand adventure. With hope in their hearts and determination in their eyes, the rats boarded the spaceship, bidding farewell to the Rat Realm. The rats of the snow Rat Realm said they would try build another portal, which would take a long time, but they hoped to see everyone again, especially Pat.

As the spaceship soared through the icy void, the rats worked together, each fulfilling their chosen jobs. Many of them powered the engines, others navigated the stars, and a few used their magical prowess to create a shield that protected them from the freezing cold.

Pat couldn't help but feel a mixture of excitement and longing. He had formed deep bonds with the rats from the Rat Realm and the future realm, but he knew he belonged in his own realm, where he had once been alone. The friendship and unity he had experienced had changed him, and he wanted to share his tales with others in his own dimension.

Days turned into weeks as they journeyed through the cosmos. They marvelled at the celestial wonders and the future rats shared stories of their unique homes.

Finally, as the spaceship reached the future Rat Realm, Pat's heart filled with a bittersweet mix of joy and sadness. The time had come for him to bid farewell to the friends he had made, he had his own dimension to return to after all. He would now be able to use the future rats' portal to travel back to his own dimension.

With a heavy but hopeful heart, Pat stepped forward, expressing his gratitude to the rats from the Rat Realm and the future realm. He promised to carry all the stories and the lessons from his new friends back to his own realm. The other rats, understanding Pat's need to return home, embraced him warmly and thanked him for the friendship and inspiration he had shared.

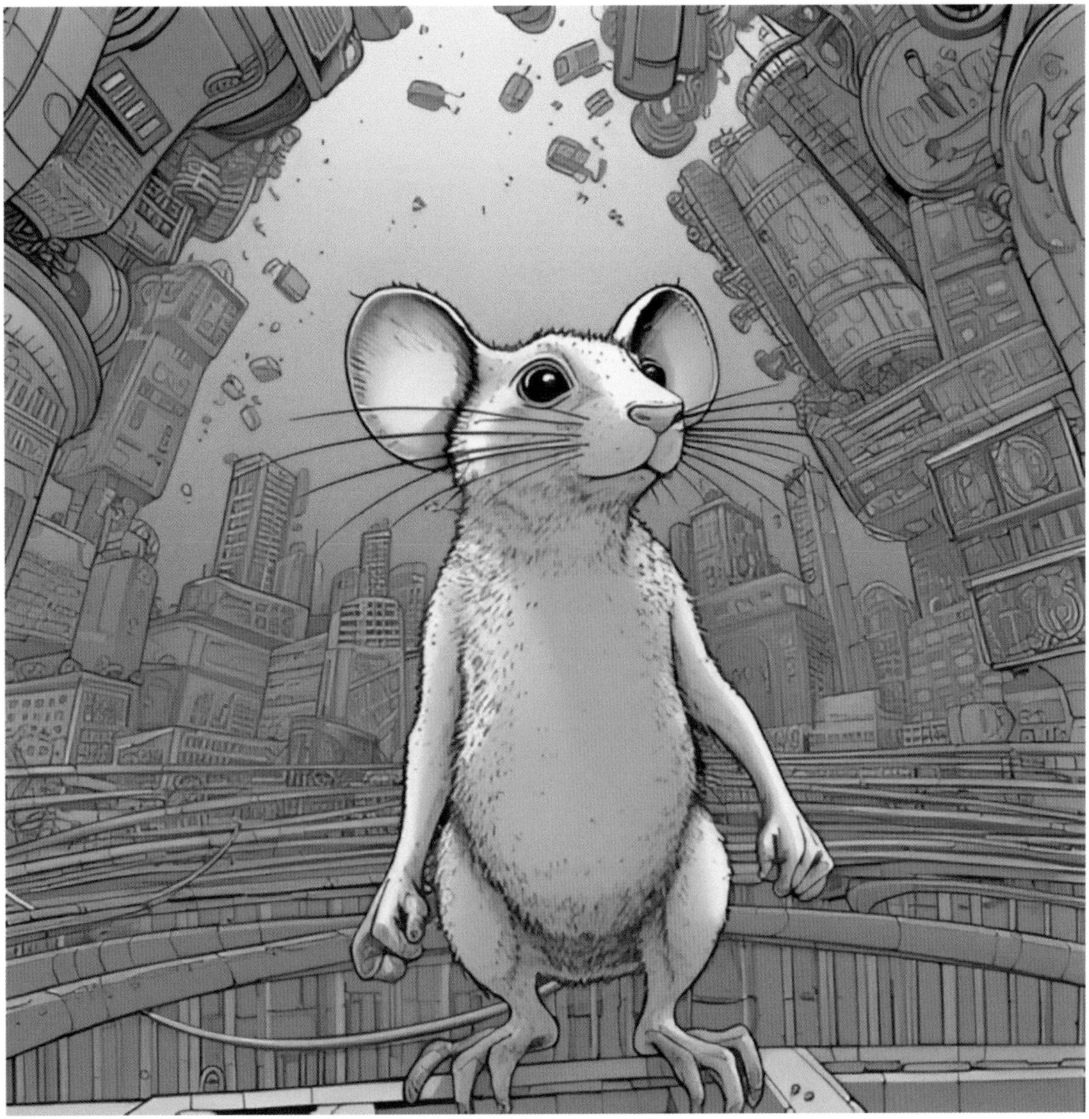

With a determined spirit, he set off on his journey back to his dimension, carrying the memories of his extraordinary adventure close to his heart. Pat leapt forward into the portal and found himself home once more.

In his own realm Pat found a new purpose. He shared his tales with his fellow rats, even the ones that hadn't accepted him before his journey, and he grew in confidence. He inspired them to dream beyond the confines of their own dimension. The legendary Pat's story was passed on to all the other rats, in the hopes that one day new legends might rise up.

Together, they formed a tight-knit community, embracing unity and friendship. And from that day forward, Pat's realm transformed into a place where rats looked out for one another, just like the Rat Realm and the future realm he had visited.

And so it was that the tale of Pat the portal-travelling rat was forged, living on through generations to follow. Paintings were made of the famous Pat and his story became a cherished one. The story taught young rats the value of unity, the power of friendship, and the beauty of exploring beyond their own horizons. And, deep within the heart of every rat, the spirit of adventure and unity would forever dwell. That spirit waiting to be awakened by the next extraordinary journey, just as it had been for Pat.

Who knows, there could be another portal opening right now.

Printed in Great Britain
by Amazon

32455572R00018